I0456308

ROAD TO KAYTLYN

MARISSA DOBSON

Copyright ©2019 Marissa Dobson
All rights reserved. No part of this publication may be reproduced, stored in a retrieval
system, or transmitted in any form or by any means, electronic, mechanical, photocopying,
recording, or otherwise, without the prior written permission of the publisher.
Published by Dobson Ink
Printed in the United States of America
ISBN-13: 978-1-946474-25-4

Dedication

To my husband. Thank you for all your support.

To my readers for everything. Without you I wouldn't be on this journey.

Chapter One

The wintery night was made worse by the winds coming off Lake Erie, sending freshly fallen snow through the air and a chill straight through Kaytlyn. This wasn't where she was supposed to be, dressed in nothing more than a little black dress and rope bidding digging into her wrists. She was supposed to be miles away in Detroit stuck in yet another so-called business event, trying to play her part as the dutiful daughter.

Dutiful daughter, that's what got me into this. A fresh wave of anger rushed through her giving her the strength to stand a little straighter. She wasn't some naïve school girl, she could find a way out of this if she kept her head.

"Ahh, there she is." A heavyset man looked her over before nodding to the man beside her, still gripping her arm.

Unlike the man holding her, this man's English was nearly perfect, only a trace of his accent lingered. Though she suspected he worked harder to blend in. In his line of work, little things such as a strong Mexican accent would have marked him in someone's memory. Things like that could link them back to a crime.

"You did well, Jorge." He spoke again pulling her from her thoughts. "Not a scratch on her. She'll fetch a good price."

"You have no idea the hell you've brought upon you and your men." Refusing to back down she met his gaze. "When my father finds out—"

"Jorge told me you're quite the handful, but he didn't tell me you were senseless." He shook his head. "Your father knows. Who do you think offered you up on a serving platter to us? He even took care of your bodyguard so we didn't have to bother with him."

"Papa would never."

"He would and he did, but believe whatever you must to get through the days ahead of you. The longer you keep your spark the longer you'll stay alive. We enjoy when it takes longer to break a woman's spirit." His smirk sent chills along her spine still she kept her gaze locked on him. "I'm Pedro, we met briefly years ago, but I doubt you remember me."

"I couldn't forget a pig like you." The words barely left her lips before his backhand met her skin. Blood formed in her mouth, but she wouldn't give him the satisfaction of knowing he'd hurt her.

Play it smart and you can survive. Let your smart comments get the best of you and it will only lead to pain. Jax's words flashed through her thoughts until the embers of rage burned brighter.

"Take her inside. She's worth nothing to me if she catches her death." He stepped aside on the deck giving them a straight shot into the house behind him. "Place her in the cell in my room. I think I'll have some fun with her before she's up on the block."

Even as comments rolled through her thoughts, she forced herself to keep her mouth shut. *Be smart, think this through, take into account every exit, every weapon you can use, and every threat.* Jax's words haunted her again but she couldn't let anger from another situation seep into this. A mistake like that could be deadly and Jax wasn't worth it. Not after all this time. Not after all he did to her, to her family.

Chapter Two

Three years in prison had left Jax Easton with one mission now that he was free—revenge. For the past three years, he had fantasized about this, putting together plans in mind for his retaliation. It wouldn't replace the years that had been snatched away from him, but it would ensure Ale Esposito would never do it again to someone else. Esposito deserved to have the things he cherished the most stripped away from him, before Jax finally ended the man's pitiful existence.

The first prize Jax set his sights on was Kaytlyn—Ale's beautiful daughter. Ale's most prized possession. Because to him, Kaytlyn was nothing more than an extension of himself. Her dreams and desires for the future meant nothing to Esposito. She was a catalyst for him to use to fulfill his own ambitions.

From their first interaction, Kaytlyn had gotten under his skin. The sweetness that radiated from her was almost enough to bring on a toothache. She didn't belong in her father's cold dark world, yet there she was surviving. The long days of prison had often been filled with thoughts of her. He wondered what she was doing. How she was surviving alongside her father, and more importantly, did she believe he was responsible for the crime that sent him to prison? That last question haunted him daily. He wanted to reach out to her, but even if it wouldn't violate the terms of his agreement with Esposito, what could he say? Nearly everyone in prison claimed to be innocent. He wasn't entirely innocent, but he wasn't guilty either, at least not of this crime. As much as he hated the in-between, he was in a gray area.

All for Kaytlyn. That's how this started and part of him knew that was how this was going to end.

"Son of a bitch!" He growled to himself as he stood hidden at the edge of the tree line. *Revenge, that's what tonight is about.* He was supposed to be kidnapping the bastard's daughter not rescuing her. Kaytlyn had been a knife in his side since he laid eyes on her, now here she was screwing his plans over again.

Even though he knew she wasn't here by choice, it seemed as though fate had decided once again to screw him over where it came to her. Not tonight. He'd get what he came for no matter the cost. All he had to do was get her out of there and his plans would be back on track. *Easier said than done.* Still, he'd never been one to give up because the challenges ahead were too steep to overcome. He'd go out fighting if the gates of Hell opened and called him home.

He scanned the lakefront home, taking in each entryway, as he searched for anyone on Pedro's payroll. While it was a tasteful home, it was on the small side compared to what he would have expected from Pedro who had

10

always preferred flashy things. Tonight, small worked, it would make things easier. A large home would have meant the possibility of too many employees. From what he could gather, it was just Pedro and the man who'd delivered Kaytlyn. Still, he had to be sure before he could make his move. Sliding his gun out of the waistband of his jeans, he neared the house, staying in the shadows. He'd find her and get them both out before anyone grew suspicious. In and out. Jax felt the adrenaline back like a familiar friend from days long ago when this used to be his life. Only now it wasn't as welcomed. Kaytlyn was at risk and that wasn't anything he'd ever wanted.

You were supposed to be kept safe, Kaytlyn. That was the promise, that was why I did the things I did. It was always for you.

Chapter Three

The cell Kaytlyn found herself in was nothing more than a very small, dark closet. Her shoulders brushed against the walls and it was barely deep enough for the empty hanger to span across before hitting the back of the closet. She never thought of herself as claustrophobic before, but this tight space made her rethink that. It was too tight for her to sit, leaving her standing in her high heel boots staring at the door.

"Think damn it, think. There must be a way out." She knew Pedro. Maybe not him personally but she knew about him and his hobbies. He sold women. Sometime as personal playthings for some rich jerk, other times the women were sold to truly evil people. The police have investigated Pedro before for sex trafficking, but nothing came from it. He kept himself isolated, letting others take the fall for him. Still she knew what he built his empire on. She'd seen first-hand what one such man had done to his prize. *I can't end up like that.* She'd rather die than be left at the hands of anyone. *Anyone besides papa, for I'm already at his mercy. I was born there and will die there. That is my life, I've accepted that, but I won't accept this.*

The top of her head brushed against a hanger as if calling to her. She snatched it off the bar by as her fingers slid over the cheap plastic. It wouldn't give her much of a weapon, but it was better than nothing. "It would have been too easy for him to have the old fashion metal ones. A weapon and a knife to cut through these ropes." Still she clung to the cheap plastic as if it was going to save her life.

Break it. Jax's voice inside her head urged her, as she readjusted her hold. If should could break it at an angle, leaving a sharp jagged edge, it might give her what she needed. All she had to do was get a good hit in and go for Jorge's gun. She could do this, more to the point, she had to do this if she wanted to keep Pedro's hands off her.

A noise caught her attention, it was almost as if there was someone breathing on the other side of the door. She hadn't heard anyone approach and even though it could have been just her imagination playing tricks on her she wrapped her fingers tighter around the hanger as she brought it up. *If you have your keys in your hand go for the eyes and bring your knee up. A solid knee to the nuts will bring any man down, no matter his size.*

Metal clicked as the key in the door turned, unlocking. Taking a deep breath, she watched as the door inched open, and prepared to make her move. Thrusting herself forward, bringing the hanger straight toward where she estimated Pedro's face should be, she fought against the blood rushing in her ears to hear if Jorge was coming. Fingers wrapped around her wrists as she brought up her knee.

"Tesoro, don't even." Still he turned, giving her his hip and denying access to his crotch.

14

Her knee brushed against his hip barely making contact as her eyes grew wide. The voice turned her mouth dry while stealing the air from her lungs. Only one person used that nickname. *Tesoro. It can't be.* The face was different, so different, and so familiar all at once. Yet it couldn't be. Her mind had to be playing tricks on her as she fought to handle the terror of what was coming.

"Tesoro." The softness of his voice had her glancing up at him. Even as she took him in, she expected reality to sink back in and find herself looking at Pedro instead.

"You can't be here. This isn't real." Shifting her wrist and forcing the tight ropes to dig into her sensitive flesh she pinched the back of her hand, half expecting to wake up from the daydream and find herself still in the closet, or worse, standing in front of Pedro. "I'm hallucinating."

"Shh Tesoro, they'll hear you." Cool metal brushed along the inside of her palm seconds before the rope dropped away. "Let's get you out of here."

"You can't be here." She reached out and touched the curve of his cheek. Feeling the cool skin under her touch she pulled back. Hallucinations aren't something you can touch, they weren't real, yet she felt him as if he was standing before her. "You're dead."

"I'm very much alive." Taking hold of her wrist he brought her hand to rest over his heart, as if feeling the beating beneath her fingers would somehow convince her all this was real.

"He said you were dead." She glanced past him, looking around the room, looking for her purse. "Where's my purse? I have your obituary."

"We don't have time for this. You have to trust that I'm alive and I'm here to protect you." With the gun still in one hand he held out the knife he'd used to cut the ropes. "Take it, just in case. You remember how I taught you to use it?"

15

"I remember." She remembered too much. His words had plagued her since this nightmare began. It was as if her mind had conjured him from memories. She needed him, so he was there just like he always said he'd be.

As he stepped away from her to check the hallway, images of her prom night filled her vision, sending her further into the past.

"My black knight." She whispered as her date hurried back inside the grand hotel, glancing back over his shoulder to ensure Jax didn't follow. "You knew I needed you and here you are."

"I'm no knight." He opened the passenger door. "Get in, I'm taking you home."

She spared one last look at the boy before turning back to the man that held her heart. "You're my knight. I'm not sure what would have happened here tonight if you hadn't showed up."

"I do. I overheard that punk bragging." His fingers tightened on the doorframe until his knuckles turned white. "Damn it, Tesoro, after everything I taught you how could you not look at that punk and know he was up to no good? What if I had not been here tonight? If your father had sent me out tonight, I wouldn't have been here. Then what? You can't just skip out on your bodyguard and not expect bad things to happen."

Standing on the other side of the door she watched him without getting in. Everyone around them disappeared, only he existed in that moment. The anger pouring off him didn't frighten her. She knew what he was capable of just as she knew he'd never harm her. Even with the impenetrable outer shell he kept firmly in place she could see something softer hidden deep inside. Sometimes it was the way he looked at her, other times it was in a conversation they shared when no one else was around. There was more to him then met the eye. Maybe that was why she agreed to his training, even though she doubted she'd need to defend herself with the guards papa always had surrounding her.

It wasn't his duty to protect her, yet he did. Whenever she was in trouble he'd been there, waiting in the wings to ride to her rescue. He was her knight. Maybe he wasn't a

16

white knight with his career choice and his signature black-on-black outfits, but he was her knight all the same.

"Why do you call me that? Tesoro? What does it mean?"

"It's Italian for treasure. You are my tesoro."

Their gazes locked and for a moment she thought he was going to kiss her. She longed for it. Dreamt about it nearly every night.

"Move." His command cut through her memory trusting her back into reality.

"You should have kissed me then and there, marked your claim for all to see. Instead you waited."

"We can talk about it later. Move now." He snapped, grabbing her wrists and pulling her toward the sliding glass doors on the other side of the room.

A gun shot exploded, sending pieces of wood through the air as the bullet imbedded itself in the trim around the door. With her ears ringing she rushed forward as Jax turned back, his gun raised.

"Look here, the little mouse has a savior." Pedro chuckled, his gun pointed at Jax but his gaze was on her. "Where do you two think you're going?"

"I'm taking what's mine and leaving."

"Yours?" Pedro let out a deep laugh. "Her father gave her to me as payment for his misfortunes. What gives you the impression she's yours?"

"She wasn't his to give. Not any longer." Jax pushed her back him, using his body as a shield. "She's been mine for longer than you've been in charge. Don't do something you'll regret."

"Jax—"

"Jax?" Pedro's eyes widened. "The infamous Jax. You made quite a name for yourself. Even running things while still confined in the penitentiary."

17

"You've heard, good, then you know what I'm capable of. Why don't you put your gun down and we'll be on our way? No harm no foul."

"That's where you're wrong. That young thing is going to fetch me quite a price. There are plenty of men who would pay a pretty penny to get their hands on Ale Esposito's daughter. Do you have any idea what they'd do to her? The things I had in mind would be nothing compared to the torture she'd endure at their mercy." His lips curled into a smile, as his eyes twinkled with the thought of her torture.

Minutes before, Pedro's words would have terrified her but with Jax at her side she stood strong. There was something about him that inspired her to have confidence that things would work out. Even when shit was hitting the fan there had to be a way out. This wasn't how things were supposed to end. She had too many unanswered questions.

Screw the questions, I want to feel his touch again. Even as the thought drifted through her mind, she knew it was only partially true. She needed to know what happened the night everything changed. Papa had told her he was dead, what else had he lied to her about. *The truth and then his mouth on mine. That's if we live through this.*

Chapter Four

With one hand on Kaytlyn's hip, Jax forced her for follow him a couple steps to the side of the sliding glass doors. Pedro's goon, Jorge was still out there somewhere and if he had made it around the lake house, Jax would be damned if he was going to give the goon an easy shot. Rather than scanning the potential outside threat Jax kept his attention on Pedro.

"Why do you think no one laid a hand on her? I've made my claim known for the very reason I know what they'd do if they caught her. She's under my protection. Anyone so much as looks at her the wrong way and they're dealt with, severely" Jax gave that a moment to sink in before continuing. "I'm feeling generous today. You didn't know of my claim to every inch of her, so I'll give you a chance to clear up this mess. Let us walk out of here without issue and we'll wipe the slate clean. Hell, maybe we can even work together, seeing we have the same target in mind."

"Esposito." Pedro tipped his head toward Kaytlyn. "You'd eliminate

Esposito?"

"Esposito and I have some long overdue business to attend to first." He felt Kaytlyn's body go still behind him, though he wasn't sure if was out of fear for her father or not. "I was there tonight to address said business when I witnessed your goon manhandle her into the back of the trunk. She's precious cargo and Jorge nearly killed her as he shoved her into the trunk of his car. Ruined my night, placed my business with Esposito on hold until another day, and risked what's *mine*. I could demand compensation from you, instead I'm offering to wipe the slate clean."

"And take what could be very profitable for me with you." Pedro reminded.

"Money cannot be spent where I'd send you if you touched her. No matter the amount you received for her it wouldn't be enough if you sold her to some other stronzo."

"Stronzo?" Pedro's eyebrow rose as he lowered the gun slightly.

"Asshole in Italian." Kaytlyn answered before Jax had the chance. "See I *do* remember."

"Interesting. You've taught Esposito's precious daughter to curse in Italian when he doesn't want her to know his native language. Does he know about that? I bet not, otherwise you'd have been dead long before you were sent to prison." Pedro let out a deep grunt before turning serious again. "You want the girl then we need to work out a deal."

"What do you want? Money? How much does he owe you?"

"Not money." As if accepting the situation Pedro lowered his gun. "A life for a life."

"Shit." It was barely above a whisper making him wonder if he even heard her correctly. "I know why I'm here and the answer is no."

"Does she speak for you now?" Pedro eyed Jax, as if watching an explosion about to happen. When Jax didn't give him the reaction he was looking for Pedro shook his head. "Here I thought Jax was a man who was up for any challenge. Your property there seems to think she controls things."

Jax didn't like the way Pedro called Kaytlyn 'his property' but to dispute that would put them back in an area of questions he didn't want to discuss. Not with Pedro, hell not with anyone other than Kaytlyn.

"I'm not exchanging myself for Jax's life." She leaned closer, pressing the front of her body tight against his back. "Please Jax, not again."

He caressed his hand over her hip, trying to convey that everything would be okay. "Why don't you tell me what you want, and we'll go from there. She believes you want me dead, but you mentioned a challenge. Even if I'd agree to exchange my life for hers, that isn't a challenge, at least not for me. So, what is it that you want Pedro?"

"Esposito murdered my son. He has no son for me to take, so he gave me his daughter. She's to birth me another son to lead when I am too old to do so. Upon the birth of my son he will regain his daughter and his debt will be cleared."

"What the hell? Papa would never—"

"Tesoro…" He kept his voice low as his fingers pressed into her hip, keeping her where she was. "He would to save his own life."

"Jax…" The pain in her voice had him glancing over his shoulder at her.

"I'm sorry, Tesoro." Needing to move this conversation forward so he could get her to safety he forced himself to look back at Pedro. "You planned to sell her though, not impregnate her."

"I have many women who would give me a child. Her…" Pedro nodded to Kaytlyn. "She's much more valuable in other ways. A son with her would risk much. I'm a cautious man I'd rather play the hand dealt to me in the most constructive way possible."

"I would rather die than give you a child. I remember your son, he was ruthless. He got himself killed."

"Kaytlyn." Jax snapped as Pedro raised his gun.

"Perhaps I've misjudged this situation. I thought of you as too soft for this life, too bendable to your fathers will, with no backbone of your own. Now I see that the spirit you had before isn't just senseless shit as I thought. You don't have the sense God gifted you to keep your mouth shut." His finger hovered over the trigger as he eyed her. "It's clear you won't live long in this world. You've only survived until now because of your father's protection. Now that he's on a slippery slide to the end, you'll fall along with him."

"Pedro." Jax shifted his weight, blocking her completely with his body. "She's been his cherished princess all her life. She doesn't understand what it takes to survive in this life. But we do. We know what must be done. You want him out of power, so the way is clear for you. That's the exchange you want, correct? I can leave with her with the promise I'll end Esposito. We can make that deal if you lower your gun."

"My son didn't get himself killed. He wasn't like you, a spoiled brat, he knew how to take care of himself." Pedro spat, still not meeting Jax's gaze.

"Because you raised him right. You raised him in our world." Hoping to de-escalate the situation Jax lowered his gun while keeping it out. "I heard about Pedro Junior. He was a good man who went down in an unfortunate situation. Your need for revenge is unquestioned. I can deliver what you ask."

"Forty-eight hours."

"You know I'm going to need longer than that." Jax shook his head.

22

"Kidnapping his princess will have him on high alert. I can use her to get close to him, but I'm going to need more than two days."

"You have until this time next week." Pedro lowered his gun as he glanced back to Kaytlyn. "Otherwise I'm coming for her and by the time you find her she'll be in pieces. Understand?"

"Crystal." Jax held out his free hand. "In return, you'll forget about Kaytlyn. You'll never come after her again or order it done. Otherwise I'll put a bullet between your eyes and anyone you send our way. Understood?"

Pedro nodded, accepting Jax's outstretched hand. "Once this job has been concluded our business will be done."

He didn't trust Pedro completely, but at that moment, he was sticking both of their necks out on the line. If things backfired, they both would end up dead, but it was the only way out of this situation. Killing Esposito had been his game plan all along. Only it had been the end goal, one that would come after some much needed revenge. Now it had been moved up. The additional hiccup to his plan was Kaytlyn was never supposed to know he intended to murder her father. *A problem for another day.*

Chapter Five

Darkness sped past as Kaytlyn at a high rate of speed as she sat in the passenger seat while Jax drove them away from Lake Erie. She didn't know where they were heading and couldn't find her voice to ask. She wasn't sure she'd like the answer even if she could. Were they heading back to the hotel where her father was supposed to be having a meeting? Had he even learned she'd been kidnapped, or did he think she just didn't show up?

"Where was Finn?"

Jax's question caught her by surprise as she turned to glance over at him. It was the first time she looked in his direction since they left Pedro's house. "Finn? You remember him? How do you know he's still my bodyguard?"

"Did you think I'd leave you unprotected?" Without slowing down, he glanced over at her.

"He's been my bodyguard since…"

"You were sixteen." He supplied. "He's still your guard, so where was he tonight?"

"Papa…" She brushed a few strands of her dark brown hair away from her face and took a deep breath. "He really handed me over to Pedro, didn't he?"

"Where was Finn? Is he still alive?" He asked ignoring her question.

"Papa called as we pulled up to the hotel. He had another guard waiting for me at the door. Plans changed, and I was now only supposed to make an appearance. Since it wouldn't take long he wanted Finn to wait in the car to be ready to leave with me when my duties were done." With her elbows resting on her knees she leaned forward to rest her head in her hands. "It was Jorge. How could I have been so stupid. I bet there wasn't even a meeting. It was all a set up to get me away from Finn, so I could be delivered to Pedro."

Jax remained silent as he pulled his cell phone out of the pocket of his jeans. While keeping a hand on the steering wheel he pressed a couple buttons on the phone.

"Finn is your man? How? He worked for my dad for years." With her head still supported by her hands she turned to look over at him. The dark interior hid most of him from view but she could see the outline of his face from the dashboard lights.

"Finn and I go way back, all the way back to our youth. He's a good man, one of the best. I knew you'd be safe with him." He dropped the phone into his lap and glanced over at her. "Once I get in touch with him, he'll get you somewhere safe. I'm going to make this okay for you."

"How?" That one question seemed to keep repeating itself over and over. Nothing about this situation felt right. It seemed like a dark hole that grew bigger and bigger with each second swallowing more of her life. There didn't seem to be any way out, any way to make it better. "By killing my father?"

"Tesoro, there is much you don't know about your father and his business. A darkness to his life that I'd hoped you would never learn. He's your father, a man you cherished and idolized most of your life, but he is not a good man."

"And you are?" She took a deep breath and leaned back. "You just spent the last few years in prison. Pedro said you've been running things from behind bars. How can you sit there and act as though you're better than him?"

"I told you before I'm no knight. I've never claimed otherwise. Still, I've never put a bullet in someone who didn't deserve it. Your precious papa can't claim that."

She sucked in a deep breath and forced herself to swallow the lump in her throat. "He can't. You say I don't realize how dark my father's world is but I know more than he thinks I do. More than you probably think I do. I know he murdered Sig, just as I know he placed the blame on you. We were cousins, but he was like a brother to me and he's dead."

"I was there that night." Jax jerked the wheel, pulling the truck over to the edge of the road before bringing the truck to a stop. "His death is on my shoulders. I should have seen what Esposito planned, should have known he'd eliminate Sig to send a message to anyone who thought of betraying him. Blood means nothing to Esposito. If someone isn't pulling their weight, doing what he needs done, he'll order their death without a second thought. He prefers not to get his hands dirty. Sig's murder was a message he had to deliver himself. That was the only way to get the full impact."

"Murder isn't the answer. It leaves families grieving and heartbroken. What does it give you in return?"

"Sig wanted to overthrow your father. He wanted to take over the family business because Esposito was becoming ruthless." He reached over placing his hand on her back. "Sig knew your father was using you to get what he wanted. He knew it would only be a matter of time before he did what he did tonight. You're a bartering chip for Esposito. You help close deals and when your usefulness runs out what do you think he'll do then?"

"He's my father." Jax's words cut through her heart, shredding it worse than any knife could. Still there was a truth in them, a truth she couldn't deny. Especially not after what happened to Sig's younger sister. "A year ago, Gianna was used to seal a peace treaty with the Kuznetsov family. Papa arranged it, against his brother's wishes. Both of my uncle's children have been taken away from him."

"I know." He caressed a hand along her back. "Sig realized what Esposito was capable of and wanted to protect you and Gianna. Taking over was the only way he could do that. Most were behind him, including your uncle. Sig's death was not enough of a message to your uncle, that's why he used Gianna to finalize the Kuznetsov deal. He didn't have to, the treaty would have been settled without her sacrifice, but she was a pawn in the greater game Esposito is playing."

Backstabbing, pawns being sacrificed for the king's enjoyment, and murder was too much for her to handle in the mist of everything else, especially considering her father was at the center of all of it. He was the king and everyone around him were sacrificial lambs, including her.

"You're going to kill him, aren't you?"

Chapter Six

Jax debated answering her question as he stared into her eyes. Esposito was responsible for a lot of her pain, for the murder of Sig and countless others, and for Gianna being in Russia. Still, the pain in her eyes made him hesitate. Every day he spent in prison, he thought about the moment he'd finally end the world of Ale Esposito. His death wouldn't bring down the Esposito family as someone else would step into his position, but it would make the world a little safer. Vic Esposito—the man who'd lead the Esposito family into the future was a different type of leader, one who wouldn't use those around him like Ale did.

Kaytlyn could hate him for the rest of his days but she'd be safe. Her safety was the one thing that matter to him. Her happiness was a close second but in this case protecting her would override all else.

"I can see it in your eyes. You will." Even as the words left her mouth, she didn't pull away from him. Rather she sat there staring at him as if she accepted it.

"Tesoro…my sweet tesoro. Protecting you has always been my priority. You have to know that by now."

"I—"

His phone buzzed, stealing her words from her. Finn's name popped onto the screen. "I've got to take this." He pulled back from her, grabbing the phone from his lap before answering it and bringing it to his ear. "Where are you?"

"She's gone." Finn's voice filled his ear.

"Where are you?" He asked again, not wanting to give Finn any information over the phone. If someone was listening, he didn't want them to know he had Kaytlyn. That was a surprise he'd save for later to avoid it getting back to Esposito.

"Buffalo, searching the area for her. It was supposed to be a short trip inside, a guard already in place but she never came out. I went into the hotel and they know nothing. I can't get their security tape without alerting Esposito that she's missing." The panic deepened his voice. "Fuck man…"

"Go to the place. I'll meet you there."

"What?" Finn raised his voice. "I'm not just leaving her."

"Trust me. I'll be there in twenty minutes." He glanced at her, debating his next words before adding. "The treasure is safe."

"The treasure…okay." The line went dead as Jax pulled the phone away from his ear.

"Treasure?" She raised an eyebrow at him.

"My tesoro, my treasure. He knows that's what I call you, he'll put it together and understand you're safe."

"How am I your treasure but you claim not to be my knight when you're

30

always there to save me?"

"Knights are good men, honorable men. That is not me." Placing his hands on the steering wheel Jax stared out the window. How could he explain to her why she deserved so much better than him? He wasn't worthy of her. She was kind and pure, where he was tainted.

"Jax…" She scooted across the seat, so she was in the middle of the truck, directly beside him, her knee brushed against the side of his leg. "You're honorable. The most honorable man I know."

"I'm going to get you out of this world and when I do, you'll realize how wrong you are. You'll find a man who will be what you deserve. A man that will be what Sig hoped you'd find when he freed you from your father's grasp."

"I found that man." She ran her hand along his thigh. "Since you came into my life at fifteen it's always been you. Five years difference is nothing now that I'm legal. I'm not the same young girl you first met. I'm an adult now. Against papa's wishes I earned my college degree in legal studies. Don't shut me out before we even have a chance."

"Legal Studies." He chuckled. "I remember when I found out you declared a major. I sat in my cell chuckling as I pictured Esposito's face when he learned this."

"I think it was our first real argument. He felt I betrayed him, betrayed our family. It was Finn who got him to see the logical side of my choice. If I was accepted into law school—which was my end goal—having a lawyer in the family could save the lives of his men. At least that's how Finn defended my decision. Even though he knew the truth."

"What's the truth?"

"I had hoped to be a prosecuting attorney. I wanted to ensure those who committed crimes were punished. I've seen my father's men get out of trouble time and time again." She let out a soft breath, shifting her gaze away from him. "Just as I've seen others go down for crimes they didn't commit. Like you."

"Tesoro, I'm a guilty man."

"Not of everything." She pulled her hand back, her gaze still on the floor instead of looking at him. "I was there. I know you didn't kill him. It was papa. I betrayed you by not standing up to my father, for not going to the police with what I saw. Because of my silence you spent three years in prison. I'm guilty—"

"No." He reached over pulling her hand into his, bringing them back into his lap. He wanted to bring her completely into his lap but with the steering wheel there wasn't enough room. "Tesoro, none of this is your fault. None. Do you understand me? I took the plea deal because I knew your father had paid people off to ensure I was found guilty. Those three years I did were nothing compared to what it would have been…I would have received the maximum penalty. He wanted me out of the way, he wanted me away from you. He knew about the night after your eighteenth birthday."

"The night." Her gaze shot up to him as a smile spread across her face. "Our night…but how? Finn?"

"Finn has been my man. He knew what was going on and he didn't report it. He's loyal…well loyal to me. As we came out of that restaurant, one of your father's guys was there on the street. I didn't have time to determine if he was following one of us or if it was a coincidence. He had to alert Esposito of what he saw. Things went down before we could handle it and I was arrested." His thumb teased along each of her knuckles as he thought about that night. Even with the consequences of those actions he wouldn't have changed a moment of it. Given the chance he'd change how things had been left between them.

"Your father visited me shortly after I was arrested. He arranged a plea deal and advised me to accept it, otherwise, he was going to ensure I received the maximum sentence. With the plea deal I'd get out of prison in a few years and could live my life again—as long as I stayed far away from you. He knew that over the years I had time to form my own group of loyal people within his structure, they were unhappy with how he was leading the family and wanted change. He wanted to avoid me using my situation to influence them further and provoke an attack. To ensure I'd take the deal he added another part. He agreed to keep you safe. He'd keep you out of harm's way and wouldn't use you as a bargain chip."

"We're not talking about a stealing from the local five and dime. This was manslaughter. Second degree manslaughter. Damn it, Jax, even with the deal it was a guarantee of at least one year in prison but you could have done ten years. Most of the evidence was circumstantial. His testimony didn't correlate with pieces of the evidence. With a good attorney you could have gotten off. If I had come to your defense—"

"It would have angered your father and he would have ensured you'd have regretted it. Ensured we both regretted your actions." His tone became enraged that she even considered this to be her fault. None of it was her doing. "Gianna's fate would have been nothing like what your father would have done to you. Even if you didn't out him as the murderer, he'd see it as a personal betrayal. I could not allow that."

"Free we could have—"

"No, Tesoro." He brought their hands to his mouth allowing the sweet scent of her lotion to tingle though his senses before placing a soft kiss on the back of her hand. "Even after everything you still underestimate your father. He'd have seen that I didn't walk out of jail alive. Six feet under in a casket wasn't going to help you. Alive, even in prison, I could ensure your safety."

"Oh, Jax…" She scooted closer to him, pressing her body along his side until he let go of her hand and wrapped his arm around her shoulders allowing her to snuggle closer. "I'm sorry."

"You have nothing to be sorry for." He pressed his lips to the top of her head.

Feeling her pressed against his body it was like nothing had changed. He still wanted her, wanted her screaming his name like she had that night before his life turned upside down. *Soon, I'll claim my tesoro again and no one will ever tear her away from me again.*

Chapter Seven

The house in East Aurora was anything but what Kaytlyn had been expecting. As Jax drove them to meet Finn, she'd expected to end up somewhere rural, further away from people, so she wasn't spotted. Rather it was a quiet middle-class town. Even the cozy three-bedroom ranch house surrounded by woods on three sides seemed out of character. It seemed lived in, homey, yet it wasn't Finn's condo and Jax hadn't been out of prison long enough to establish this, leaving her unsure of who's house they were in.

"Why don't we go into the living room? I started a fire and I already have a pot of coffee sitting in there." Finn suggested.

"This isn't your place though. Is it?" She glanced at the man she come to trust over the years.

"It's mine." Jax touched her shoulder. "Finn has been looking after it for me, staying here more than at his own condo. Since my release it's become our headquarters."

"When papa learns you have me, he'll come here."

"That would be his first move if he knew I owned this house. He doesn't and the only one on his staff that has the computer skills to dig deep enough to unveil the truth behind the hidden names is no longer loyal to Esposito."

"Salvador…" She turned to face him. "He's weak, scared of his own shadow. All father has to do is threaten him in the right way and he'll crack."

"Old Sal has more of a backbone than he lets on. He's been working with your uncle for years, alerting him to anything that might be of interest." Jax rubbed his hand down her back. "Trust me."

"He's right. Sal is a good man he'll do what's right because he knows what's at risk. He wants Vic Esposito in charge as much as the rest of us." Finn nodded toward the opening to the living room. "Come sit, Kaytlyn, you've had a long night and it's only going to get longer."

"I'm sorry…" She stepped away from Jax, crossing the entryway to stand near Finn. "You spent hours searching for me, no doubt concerned for my safety as well as what the future would hold."

"Stop." Jax ordered coming up behind her. "You're always so worried about everyone else. You were the one kidnapped and you're apologizing that he had to do his job. If I'd still been behind bars, he'd have been your best chance at getting out of Pedro's hands alive."

"I know." She shifted to the side allowing her to look at Jax. "Finn has been my bodyguard for years. He's gotten me out of situations I wasn't sure I'd survive. I'm thankful to have him by my side, to have both of you."

"Don't apologize." Finn's words had her turning back to him. "I wouldn't have given up until I found you."

"That's why he's your bodyguard." Jax nodded. "Go sit. I need to make a call and I'll join you."

"Come on." Finn nodded. "I just so happen to have some of those fancy cookies you like."

"Just happen to?" Her lips curled into a smile. "Couldn't be because you enjoy those fancy butter cookies just as much as I do?"

"Never." He teased even though they both knew he picked up the craving for those cookies because of her nerves. After years of offering him a cookie he had given into her to prove she could score high enough to get into the law school of her choice.

"Come on, Finn!" She sat on the edge of the kitchen counter, her legs swinging back and forth as she held out one of her favorite cookies to him. "Just try one bite. I promise you won't regret it."

"I don't like fancy cookies." He leaned against the counter across from her, his arms crossed over his black shirt.

"Now finish your disgusting snack so we can get going."

"Try one." She leaned closer, cookie still held out to him. "It will be good luck for my test. Come on, Finn, this exam will determine everything."

"Not everything." He shook his head. "You can retake it."

"Everything." Dropping her hand into her lap she looked down at the cookie, suddenly no longer interested in her favorite treat. "I need to do well in order to get into law school. If my score isn't high enough, I'm done. Papa will never agree to me taking it again. I can't believe he even allowed me to take it in the first place."

"A lawyer in the family is good business for him." Avoiding her swinging legs, he stepped closer, and placed his hand on her wrist. "You've been studying nonstop for more than a month now. You're prepared for the test. Stop worrying and let's do this."

"You think?"

"I know." He plucked the cookie out of her hand and brought it to his mouth. "For good luck and just for you." With a smile he popped the cookie into his mouth. The moment

the sweet buttery cookies hit his tongue his eyes widened.

"Good, aren't they?" She smirked, hoping over the counter. "I knew you'd like them."

"Finn…" Her voice low as she dropped onto the plush tan sofa, exhaustion from the recent events catching up to her.

"Yeah?" He pressed when she remained silent.

"Jax's going to kill my father." The words should have sent anger or fear running through her instead she was hollow, empty of emotion. "Shouldn't I be upset about this? Shouldn't I want to save my father? Why do I feel as if I'm already grieving?"

"I haven't gotten the story as to why you disappeared from the hotel or how you ended up with Jax but I can put together enough to know this…"

He handed her a package of their cookies and sat on the chair beside the sofa before pouring her a mug of coffee. "Esposito was responsible for your disappearance tonight. Otherwise he'd have called to find out where you were when you didn't show up in the meeting. I checked the hotel and there was no meeting. Esposito wasn't there tonight…hell he hadn't been there in months from what I gathered from the staff. It was a set up and the only reason I can think of is to get you out of the way. I'm sorry, Kaytlyn, but that's the only way this pans out. Esposito knew Jax was released from prison, he knew Jax would want to see you even though he wasn't supposed to. And when you found out he was alive, everything your father has done would have been exposed. Esposito couldn't let that happen. Not when Jax would risk everything for you. You know that don't you?"

"I know." Lifting one of the cookies from their metal tin she held it out to Finn. "Papa gave me to Pedro as payment for killing Pedro Junior. I was supposed to give Pedro another son and then be returned to my father but Pedro had other plans."

38

"Selling you to the highest bidder." Finn took a cookie but didn't bring it to his mouth. "Pedro has a harem of women, why would he want you to carry his child? It would only bring problems for him later."

"Papa was playing the long game." She sat the tin of cookies aside and leaned back against the sofa. "Our son would be used to unite the two families. Papa would see it as a power move, he would write off the risks because his family is bigger. Their trades are different with Pedro focusing on sex and drugs while Papa prefers guns and loan sharking. It would expand his empire. He'd use me just as he used Gianna with the Kuznetsov family."

"He's your father but in your heart, you know he can't remain in power." His words were gentle but they tightened her chest all the same.

"I know." The first tear rolled down her cheek as her heart shattered again. "He sold me tonight to save himself, and that angers me, but what infuriates me is that he lied to me. He told me Jax was dead. I have a fucking obituary that was supposed to prove he was dead. I grieved for him and you…you let me. How could you, Finn?"

"I knew this was coming." He ran his hand through his shoulder reddish-blond hair before meeting her gaze. "I struggled with that decision every day. At the time it seemed the right thing to do. Esposito knew Jax was getting out of prison soon and he wanted to end anything before it started. Having you think Jax was dead would ensure you didn't go looking for him after his release."

"You could have, no you should have, told me the truth." The rage pulsed within her forcing her to sit her uneaten cookie aside before the flakey goodness ended up in nothing more than crumbs.

"The grief needed to be real, otherwise Esposito would have known you knew the truth. It would have put you at risk." He shook his head as if angry with himself. "It's not an excuse, but I said a couple little things that should have made you suspect it was a lie. I had to be careful because it would have put us both at risk. Maybe I didn't try as hard as I should have, but I knew in a few months you'd find out the truth. You could hate me if you wanted but you'd be safe when Jax got out and that's what mattered."

"He did what I asked him to do." Jax's announcement had her turning to look over the back of the sofa as he strolled into the living room coming straight for her. "Neither of us liked the idea but he's right, you were safe, and the grief had to look real."

"Why? Shouldn't I have already grieved for you?" She let her anger vibrate through her as she eyed him. "You ripped my heart out when I came to see you after you accepted the plea deal. If that wasn't bad enough, you tore it to shreds before standing up from the booth and walking away from me."

"For you—"

"For me! That's all I ever hear." She snapped rising off the sofa in one quick movement. "Why don't I ever get a say in what's done for me? Why do the men that surround me think they can make all the decisions and I'll just fall in line? I'm tired of it."

"Kaytlyn." Finn stood but stayed near his vacated chair. "We want to protect you. It started as my job but overtime you've come to mean as much to me as Jax does. You're family. We're family, all of us. Maybe none of us by blood but we're still family. Family protects one another."

"He's right." Jax closed the distance between them. "Finn and I met years ago in the system—group home for trouble boys. My folks where murdered when I was seven, where as his decided he wasn't worth the trouble he caused. We bonded over the shit deal we were given and wreaked havoc

40

where we could. Esposito knew our history and if your grief wasn't real he'd know Finn was the one who told you the truth. It would have made our plans to keep you safe harder. Finn would have been taken off your guard detail and possibly killed for his betrayal. It would have made you more determined to see me when I got out. All around it would have made things more difficult than they had to be. I needed things to go smoothly so I could get you away from Esposito."

"Get me away? What does that even mean?" Emotions jumbled within her she wasn't sure how to handle all of this at one. Where the two men she trusted more than anyone else actually traitors? "Why were you even there tonight? Were you going to kidnap me?"

"If kidnapping is what it took, then yes I'd have done that." Jax nodded.

"Wow!" She took a step back only to find there was nowhere else to go. Pressed against the sofa she sank back onto the cushions again. "I trusted you...I trusted both of you."

"Finn was aware I was released, but he didn't know I would be there tonight. He knew my end goal was to release you from Esposito's hold, but he didn't know I planned on coming for you tonight, or even in the coming days. I kept that to myself because I knew he'd talk me out of it. Part of it was I needed to see you, to explain, but I also wanted you away from your father." Jax squatted down in front of her, not touching her but bringing them to the same level. "Kidnapping you was an option, if that's what it took to get you away from Esposito, but I had hoped you'd come with me willingly. For years revenge against your father plagued me, but more than that it was all for you. I wanted you safe and as long as you were under his roof and his thumb you weren't safe."

"You were the reason I continued to work for Esposito, the reason I brought Finn into this shit. I needed someone to watch over you, to keep you safe when I couldn't be there. Finn was that man. I trust him with my life. More importantly, I trust him with your life and that, Tesoro, is so much more valuable to me."

"If that's true why did you say the things you said to me at the jail? You sent me away."

"Who did you bring with you that day?" Jax questioned.

Memories of that day flooded back to her, filling her vision and transporting her back in time.

Standing in front of the metal bars waiting for them to open and allow her into the visiting room she glanced back over her shoulder, Aldo stood a few steps away, his gaze on her. Jax was only allowed one visitor, which mean Aldo, had to wait there, but she was still in his line of sight. He'd only agreed to it because there'd be a plexiglass divider between them. Jax and she could talk on the phone and see each other, but they couldn't touch. She longed to touch him, to feel his fingers run along her skin again, but for now this would have to do.

"It's better than not seeing him at all." She mumbled to herself as she was led into the room.

"Fourth booth." The guard ordered

Her heart raced as she sat down. Seconds passed, each one feeling like hours as she waited for him to appear. As he stepped through the door, tears sprang to her eyes. The orange jumpsuit fitting tight across his chest was so different from his usual black that it brought a smile to her face. Her heart raced as her gaze moved up, traveling along his face before meeting his gaze. His eyes were cold, anger rolling off him as he dropped down to the metal stool and snatched the phone from the hook.

"What the fuck are you doing here?"

"Ja—"

42

"You don't belong here, princess." The last word nearly spat at her slicing deep within her.

"I wanted to see you."

"Why? You've seen a murderer before."

"You didn't ki—"

"Shut your mouth." He snapped. *"You know nothing of what happened. Spoiled little princess thinks she knows how the world really works but she knows shit."*

"What happened to you?" She shook her heard trying to make sense of the sudden change in his attitude. He never spoke so harshly to her or looked at her with such anger. Didn't he know she'd been there that night?

"Being sentenced to prison will harden anyone."

"Answer me." Jax's demand pulled her back into reality.

"I'm not a spoiled princess." The words escaped her lips on a whisper before she could regain her grip on reality. "Damn it Jax, that's twice you've called me his princess, but I've never been that. A pawn yes, but not a princess. That's always been a show for others. He's kept a tight grip on me making sure I obey every command."

"I know." Jax nodded. "I treasured you more than your father every did. Now answer me, who came with you that day?"

"Aldo."

"One of your father's most loyal men. Do you think that was by accident?" Jax shook his head before she could answer. "No, he wanted someone to report back to him that I turned you away. Esposito needed to know I was keeping the deal. Otherwise you'd have been fair game for him to do whatever he wanted."

"But Finn…" She glanced over Jax's shoulder to where Finn stood. "You were supposed to go with me."

43

"Esposito sent me out on a mission the night before to pick up a shipment of weapons. It was unusual for me to do those kinds of runs since I was your primary guard, but he claimed to be a man short. I should have been back in plenty of time, but the crate wasn't set to arrive until morning. When I called, he claimed to have misread the schedule. He'd have someone cover my shift. Without me mentioning it he assured me they'd reschedule the jailhouse visit because he wanted someone he could trust protecting his daughter." Finn shook his head. "Stupid me. I believed him. When I got back, I checked on you and found out what happened."

"It was all set up to put Aldo in place as your guard that day. With him there, I had no choice." Jax explained. "If it had been Finn, I could have been gentler."

"Gentler?" She let her attention return to Jax.

"Even if it had been Finn, I need to make sure you didn't come back. I didn't want you to see me in there and every time you had any communication with me, through letter or visit it would have put you at risk. If Esposito found out he'd have taken it as a violation of our agreement. He'd have used anything he could to keep you as his pawn."

"Seems I'm a pawn in everyone's games." She shook her head. "I'm assuming you're not going to let me leave, so is there a place I can rest?"

"Do you want to leave?"

She shifted her gaze back to Jax who was still squatted in front of her. He seemed too still, as if waiting for her to demand to be returned home. He seemed unsure of her answer, making her want to say something reassure him, but how could she when she didn't even know what she wanted?

"I don't know." Part of her didn't want to leave, not after she finally had Jax there with her. The other part despised the idea that she was a pawn for him as well. His motives might be true, but he was still using her in a way to get back at her father.

Chapter Eight

In the middle of a plush bed, surrounded by more pillows than one person could ever need, Kaytlyn couldn't sleep. Her thoughts were racing faster than she could narrow them down. It had been like that for more than an hour since she'd curled up on the bed. She laid there listening to the house, hoping to hear something that would let her know what would happen next which was impossible.

Jax and Finn were in Jax's office, plotting out their next move. Last she heard, they were trying to determine if Esposito believed Pedro still had her. They had already put together a plan to make Finn's absence understandable, giving them an inside man if they still needed it. Even knowing they were putting together a plan to kill her father she continued to lay there, unmoving, as the two sides of her heart warred over her own future moves.

A good daughter would warn him of the assassination plans. Doing that would put her back into a situation with Pedro or worse. Papa wouldn't stop until he reached his end goal. Using her was nothing to him, just as he used Gianna.

She could go to her Uncle Vic. Maybe he could figure out a better plan. Even though Jax had told her Uncle Vic was on their side, she had her doubts. Vic and her father were brothers, as far as she could see Vic always respected her father, even after everything that had happened.

No matter my move I'm going to lose someone. I just have to decide who I'm willing to give up. My black knight or the man who sold me into slavery to save himself.

Pushing back the covers she scooted out of bed. Without bothering to find anything more to wear than the shirt Jax had given her to sleep in she padded down the hall toward Jax's office. She needed to talk to him.

"You sure you want to do this?" Finn's question stopped her in her tracks.

"I have to." Jax let out a soft breath. "For Kaytlyn, for my parents, Sig, Gianna, and everyone else who suffered horrible fates at his hands."

"You sure he's the one."

"No doubt. That fucking bastard told me when he visited me in jail. *I should have killed you that night too. Instead of being grateful I let you live you repay me by fucking my only daughter. She'd have fetched me quite a penny as a virgin, but you had to fuck it up.* Every time I close my eyes, I can still hear those words. He always knew who I was. To him it was justice to have me working for him when my parents refused his offer."

"And betrayal when you bedded his daughter." Finn added.

My father killed his parents? With the air sucked from her lungs she took a step back, not wanting to alert them of her presence. As she did she bumped the hall table, causing it to bang off the wall. *Shit!*

Gun drawn Jax stepped into the hall, Finn close behind him, searching for the intruder.

With no other choice she raised her hands and stepped out of the shadows. "I'm sorry…"

"Fuck, Tesoro." Jax lowered his gun to slid it back into the holster on his hip as he came closer. "You could have gotten yourself shot."

"Why didn't you? I mean why don't you?" She shook her head, unsure how to phrase what was on her mind. "He killed your parents…"

"Oh, Kaytlyn." He wrapped his arm around her and brought her close to him.

"I'll get things ready. You deal with this, then get some rest." Finn glanced at her before heading back into the office.

"Come on." With his arm around her shoulders he led her back the way she came, toward the bedroom he had offered her.

"We need to talk."

"No, what you need is sleep." His arm slid down her back until it was wrapped around her waist. "You're upset and it's been a rough day. Rest and we can talk in the morning."

Stepping into the bedroom suite she glanced at the bedside table clock. "It's already morning."

"Two in the morning doesn't count and you know that's not what I meant." He drew her in front of him, so they were looking at each other. "I know you, you need to think things through. To overthink every option and then reanalyze everything again. You can't do that if we're talking."

"Fine." She looped her arms around his neck. "Forget the talking. Come to bed with me."

"Kaytlyn." His voice was deep, warning her.

"Don't use that tone with me." She tanged her fingers in his hair at the

49

base of his neck. "It's been a long time...a long time for both of us. Let me be your first after...well you know."

"Who say I haven't fucked my way around town since I got out?"

"I know you, Jax. Fucking and one-night stands have never been your thing. Not even prison could have changed that. Not with you." She bit her bottom lip. "We both need this. Let tonight be our night because tomorrow I don't know what will happen."

"One night wasn't enough before." With his arm still around her waist, he tugged her closer, pressing her against the front of his body, she could feel his heartbeat. "It won't be enough this time either."

"That's what I'm counting on." She stared up into his eyes. "My black knight, I love you. I always have."

"Don't, Tesoro." Barely above a whisper as he leaned forward until he rested his forehead on hers.

"We both know it's true. I started falling in love with you the first day you walked into my life. You were my first crush, my first partner, and my first love. You were the hardest to get over, the one I'd never forget. Dead or alive you held my heart. I need you to know that."

"Fuck baby, you're going to be the death of me." His lips brushed hers, not yet claiming them.

"I want to be your life. Not your death." She closed the distance claiming his mouth before he could respond.

She wasn't the same woman she had been when they first had sex, but she was still his in every way that mattered. There had never been anyone else. He had been the only one her mind and soul wanted. The only one her body responded to.

He broke the kiss and lifted his chin toward the bed. "You asked for it.

Now get on the bed."

"I'll beg for it if that's what's needed." She took a step back from her, tugged his shirt over her head and shot him a cocky smile. "Like what you see?"

"Tesoro, you know I do. I'm going to fuck you until you're hoarse from screaming my name."

"What are you waiting for?" She hopped onto the bed and leaned back against the pillows. "Come here my black knight."

"Tesoro." His voice held warning, but his grin never faded.

"If I'm your tesoro, you're my black knight. Want to negotiate? I'm willing to accept white knight, perhaps just knight."

"One day I'll prove I'm worthy of your pet name." He stripped out of his clothes as he made his way toward her.

"You already have." She assured him as she reached across the edge of the bed to run her fingers along the perfect contours of his abs. "Damn…"

"There's not much to do in prison." He slipped into place on top of her, she brought her legs up on either side of him and lazily dragged one hand along the side of his chest. Her fingers teased along his ribs but it was the contour of his muscles that she was enjoying. The tight muscles contracted under her touch, showing off the beauty of his chest. He worked hard to bulk up and she admired it.

"You were always fit but this…" She looked up into his eyes. "It makes me want to run my tongue over every contour, every indent, and every peak. I'm glad we've got all night."

"Here I thought you said it was already morning." He teased.

"And I thought you were going to make me scream your name. Guess we're all a little confused here." She dragged her nails along his skin. "Get to work black knight, you're not leaving this bedroom until I'm hoarse and completely satisfied."

"Oh, you will be." He teased the tip of his dick along her slit before he arched forward, shoving it into her pussy in one quick movement, clearly telling her conversation time was over. All he wanted out of her was moans and her screaming his name.

A moan tore from her chest as her core muscles stretched to accommodate his width. "Jax!" Breathlessly, she ran her hands up his chest as her body quickly adjusted to his invasion.

"That's right, Tesoro, scream my name."

Staring down at her, he slowly pumped his hips, sliding his dick in and out of her. Using one arm to keep himself hovered above her, he brought his other hand to her breast. He groaned as his fingers found her hard nipples. Rolling the hardened bud between his fingers, pinching it with enough pressure to have her arching forward, he increased his pace. Each pump of his hips had him going harder and faster, stealing her breath as her climax neared. Heat coiled between her thighs and her sex clenched around him.

"Please…faster!" She lifted her body up to meet his.

"You feel so fucking good wrapped around my dick. I've missed this." He pulled nearly his full length out, before slamming back into her. When he did, he sped his pace up. Their bodies rocked back and forth, each thrust gaining momentum, drawing her closer to her orgasm.

"So close. Please…" As if knowing what she needed to push her over the edge, he slid his hand between them, his thumb instantly finding her clit. Clearly not enough for him as he dipped his head, his lips wrapping around her nipple to suck it in between his teeth. He swirled his tongue around the bud before his teeth closed down around it.

"Oh…" she hissed in a mixture of pain and pleasure. Her climax was almost upon her as she arched forward, sending his dick deeper into her.

"Look at me. I want your eyes on me. I want you to know it's my dick in you, bringing you to your orgasm." His voice sounded strained as if he was close to his own orgasm but wouldn't give in until she had her release first.

"Jax," she whispered, her climax within reach. "Faster, please…" Her nails raked down his chest.

With one last flick over her clit, he leaned back, placing both hands on her hips, and pounded into her faster. She wrapped her legs around him, locking her ankles together at the small of his back, which kept him from pulling back too far. Tension had her muscles constricting around him as her orgasm neared, urging him to engage an even faster rhythm, and his eyes glazed over with his own ecstasy creeping up on him.

Keeping her gaze locked on his, she pressed her body to his. Her fingers tangled in his longer strands, bringing his head down so she could claim his lips. Slipping her tongue in between his lips, she moaned his name as her release found her. With her free hand, she raked the skin along his chest, digging her nails into his flesh.

Her core muscles tightened around him and she could feel the tension release from him as he slammed into her one final time before leaning forward against her and letting go, filling her. He buried his face in the arch of her shoulder. "Fuck, Kaytlyn."

"Mmm…now I know I can't ever let you go. Not again." With her fingers still in his hair, she let the palm of her hand brush along the side of his face. Her muscles continued to tighten around him, milking his cock for every drop. "My black knight, you might not want to hear it, but I love you."

"My sweet tesoro, you've owned my heart for as long as I can remember.

I wasn't worthy of you before and I'm still not, but I'll live every day trying to be the man you need. I love you."

The idea of spending the rest of her life with him sent her heart fluttering. It was what she'd always wanted but thought she lost when he went to prison. Even through that there was a ray of hope she'd find a way back to him, up until the obituary. *I can't lose you again.*

Chapter Nine

Cuddled next to Kaytlyn, Jax enjoyed the after-sex bliss, trying not to consider what the coming hours or even days had in store for them. There was much to do in order to keep her safe. He still wasn't sure how handling her father would affect what was happening between them. There was no doubt in his mind that killing Esposito would affect things. He expected she'd hate him, just as he despised Esposito for killing his parents.

"Why did he kill your parents?" Her fingers teased along his chest as she shifted to look up at him. "I mean if you don't mind me asking."

"It was a shakedown gone bad. My father owned a small market here in East Aurora. Esposito had a set up with the previous owner, money for protection. My dad wanted nothing to do with it. He believed in protecting his own. We lived above the shop, it wasn't much but it was home. Esposito burned the place to the ground, killing everyone inside. My parents and younger sister. I should have been there." The memory brought back the stench of smoke, chard wood, and burning flesh, nearly making him gag again. Turning his heard to bury his face in the top of her head, filling his senses with the sweetness of her shampoo he pushed the memory away.

"How old was she?"

"Four." His sister's face popped in front of his eyes like a movie projector. Her sweet brown eyes taking everything in and nearly black hair sticking up everywhere as if she put her finger in the electrical socket. "She was the sweetest child you'd ever meet. From the beginning she was a joy. She rarely cried except when she was hungry or needed her diaper changed. If one of us had to survive it should have been her."

"Don't do that." Her hand caressed along his cheek until he looked down at her. "I'm sorry, so sorry."

"None of this is your fault, you were just a toddler when it happened, even if you weren't it still isn't your fault. He made the decision, he fucking lit the match." With a deep breath he added. "I never understood why he let me live that night. He knew who I was and saw me coming from the shop, heading up the street to a friend's house to play, and he let me go."

"Maybe it had to be you…it had to be you here fighting to take him down."

"So, I could lose the only person I've loved since I lost them?" He shook his head. "That's some fucked up karma if I ever heard some."

"No." She propped herself up on her elbow, so she could look down at him. "I love my father, but he has to be stopped. Too many people have died because of him, too many lives ruined. Look at our families. Yours died because of him. Uncle Vic lost both of his children, Sig is dead, and Gianna is married off to a Russian family to make peace between us. These are people, they're not cattle or pawns. They have their own hopes and dreams."

"Are you…" Needing her to say it herself he let the question go unasked.

"I'm not saying you should kill him, though I understand why you want to. Isn't there another way? Removing him from power should keep people safe."

"But not you." He shook his head. "Pedro will come after you until I follow through. I can't allow that to happen."

"I was there when you made the deal, I remember what was said. You said remove him from power, so Pedro's way was clear. That can still happen without killing my father." She pulled back from him further. "If are you doing this for your parents say so, don't you use me as an excuse."

"It started out as revenge for them. Hell, even for me while I was in prison. But when it all boils down to the main reason I keep fighting, it's you. Fuck, Kaytlyn. I love you and I want to protect you. I can't stand the thought of something happening to you."

"Why can't we try it my way? Remove him from power and have Uncle Vic take over. You can always kill him later. Or Pedro can. Though I think we can make this work if we try. You know we can."

"Finn is contacting Vic about a meeting in the morning. We'll discuss it and get their take on it." His hand slid down her body. "Since you're able to do this much talking I don't think you're hoarse enough. Come here, I'm ready for round two."

Chapter Ten

With a grin on her face Kaytlyn cocked an eyebrow at him. "Oh, really now?"

"Yes, and I want you on top." Taking hold of her hips he shifted her up on top of him, she worked with him, careful to avoid his already rock-hard cock.

"Giving up control. I didn't expect that from my black knight."

"I like to keep you on your toes, make sure you never know what to expect. Are you up for the challenge?" His fingers teased along her hip before moving up her torso.

"You know I am." Not wasting a moment, she adjusted so she was in a better position as she straddled his hips and wrapped her hand around his shaft. Gliding caresses up and down the hard length, she teased his erection harder. He groaned and reached up to caress her breasts. Heat coiled between her thighs and her sex clenched.

"I can't get enough of you. I've waited so long for to have this again. To have you again."

"It hasn't even been an hour." He playfully slapped her ass.

"You know what I mean." She loved the feel of him in her hand and knowing she caused his cock to be rock hard. It proved he desired her as much as she wanted him.

"We've got as long as you'll have me."

"Forever then." She shot him a grin, even though in her gut she knew forever might end in hours. Murdering her father could send him back to the very place he was just released from, or worse put him in the ground, six feet under.

"Forever." He echoed.

Needing to get out of her head away from the thoughts of the future that plagued her, she shifted her position, angling the head of his cock just below her opening. Slowly almost painfully slow she sank down onto it, allowing his hardness to fill her inch by inch, until his low moan echoed hers. Sliding his hands up her body until he found the underside of her breast. Cupping her breasts, he pinched her nipple allowing the pain to mingle with pleasure. She rocked upward and then down again, finding her rhythm. Impatience coiled through her as she tried to find the right motion. As if realizing her frustration, he grasped her hips, increasing his pace and driving into her with force.

With every thrust, he sped his pace, hands on her hips, pulling her down onto him harder and faster. Stroke after stroke, the tempo between them intensified until his hips where slamming off hers. The thrusts became deeper, more urgent, falling into a perfect rhythm. Their bodies rocked back and forth and her back arched, pushing her breasts out toward him as her orgasm neared. The tension strained through her muscles, tightening around his cock.

"Fuck." He dug his fingers into her hips. "Tighten around my cock. Damn, Kaytlyn, I love it when you do that."

As she pushed down onto him, he arched up to meet her. Even faster and deeper, they met each other's thrusts. They climbed the mountain, both seeking the apex. "Jax!" Screaming his name, she slammed down onto his body as her orgasm found her. She dragged her nails along his chest, leaving angry red scratches.

His grasp on her hips tightened, keeping his cock buried deep within her as his own orgasm hit him. "Fuck, Tesoro."

She collapsed on top of him, her hands on either side of him, holding him tight to her. Staring down at him she remember how many times she dreamed about having this moment again, now that it was here, fear flooded through her. She was terrified it would all end again, just as it did last time. They shared their time together and then he was snatched away from her without so much as a goodbye. It broke her heart and her spirit until she wasn't sure how she managed to continue living.

I can't survive that again.

"Tesoro." He brushed her hair away from her face.

"Sorry." The word came out on a broken whisper as she tried to push the fears away and move off him.

"No." He wrapped his arms around her, holding her in place. "You're staying right there until you tell me what's wrong."

"Then I'll stay." She wrapped her lips over his nipple, gently biting it.

"Fuck." His cock twitched inside her, sending a jolt of desire rushing back through her, forcing her inner core muscles to tighten around him again. "Tesoro, if you do that again, I won't be responsible for my actions."

"What will you do?" She teased, needing him to distract her enough to keep her thoughts away from the past.

"Are you testing me?" He swatted her ass, making her jerk in surprise. "It's been a long time. With a couple minutes I'll be ready to go again, and I'll roll you over and fuck you again. Tomorrow you'll be so fucking sore you can't walk straight, let alone sit."

"Oh, Jax!" She slipped off him to cuddle beside him. "This is the life. I want to wake up every morning next to you and have amazing sex like this every night. Only then will my life would be complete. Still if morning comes and you regret this or if something happens we will always have tonight to remember."

"Morning is already here, and I won't regret this not today, tomorrow, or next week. I'll prove it to you by staying up until the sun rises if that's what it takes." He pressed his lips to her forehead. "I thought of you every single day and dreamt about you every night. I love you, Kaytlyn Esposito. Somehow we'll make a future for us."

Happiness bubbled within her as excitement for the future tightened her chest. Even with the battles that no doubt waited for them they'd have each other. That would give them the strength to get through everything that waited for them.

Chapter Eleven

With the morning light came new problems awaiting Jax, all before he even had his first sip of coffee. When they'd finally fallen asleep he'd pictured waking her up to another round of sex. Instead Finn's knocking aroused them both from a deep slumber.

"Vic is here." Finn glanced over Jax's shoulder toward the king bed where Kaytlyn sat wrapped in nothing but the blanket. "It's urgent, he's requesting both of you."

With a nod Jax shut the door, turning back to Kaytlyn. "Get dressed. Your uncle is here."

"What's he doing here already?" She scurried to the edge of the bed going for the black dress she wore the night before.

"Wait." Ignoring her question, he disappeared into the closet, quickly going to the stash of clothes Finn had purchased for her in case they ended up there together. He grabbed an ivory sweater and black jeans, along with underwear and bra. "Here."

"Whose clothes are these?" She stared at them without taking them from him.

"Yours. Well Finn purchased them upon my request." He dropped the clothes into her hands before turning back to the closet to find his own items.

"He what? Why?"

"I knew you'd end up here one way or another. I wanted to be prepared." He glanced back over his shoulder at her. "If you'd rather wear the dress from last night feel free."

"Cocky asshole."

"You love this cocky asshole. You said so yourself." He tugged on a pair of black jeans before grabbing a long sleeve black shirt to match. "Whatever brought Vic here early is urgent. If you rather nit-pick about clothes, you'll have to do it by yourself."

"Damn you're grumpy with little sleep." She let out a huff. "I only asked because I'm not wearing one of your hookers' outfits."

He spun around on her, finding her half-dressed, and pressed her against the wall. "There are no other women in my life. There hasn't been in a long time. Hell, long before I went to prison. You spoiled them for me. No one could compare to you."

"Jax—"

"Don't." He warned pressing his lips to hers in a hungry kiss. His tongue slipped between her lips before she could protest. The sweater fell to the floor as she wrapped her arms around him, drawing their bodies closer. "I'd like nothing more than to give you what you crave but Vic is waiting."

"After." That simple word held a promise from her he wasn't sure she'd be able to keep.

"Let's go." He stepped back from her allowing her to grab the sweater and pull it over her head as he finished tugging his own shirt on.

Leaving the bedroom, he slipped her hand into hers, interlacing their fingers. Together. Whatever this was about they were going to face it together.

"I assure you they're coming." Finn's voice carried down the hallway toward them.

"Seems Vic is growing impatient." He spared a glance over at her as they rounded the counter.

"Uncle Vic is never like this." Her worried gaze met his. "Something's wrong."

"We'll handle it together." He squeezed her hand as they neared the living room.

"Together." She whispered as they rounded the corner.

"What's taking them so—"

"Uncle Vic." She called as they came into the room.

"Kaytlyn." He spun back to look at her. "There you are."

"What's going on, Vic?" Jax held her hand keeping her at his side.

Vic was on their side because they wanted the same things. It didn't mean Vic wouldn't betray them if it meant getting Ale out of the picture anyway. Until he knew what this urgent visit was about, Kaytlyn needed to stay where he could protect her.

"Ale's dead." Vic dragged a hand through his short black hair and turned to look at them.

For the first time Jax was able to take the other man in. The dark circles under his eyes, the blood splatter on the front of his shirt and the haunted look in his eyes.

"What have you done?" Kaytlyn asked before Jax could process what Vic had said.

"Me!" Vic spat his anger turning toward her. "You started this in motion. Both of you."

"How?" Kaytlyn pulled her hand out of his and stepped forward. "My father sold me to Pedro to save his own ass. The only reason I'm not tied to his bed or sold to the highest bigger is because Jax rescued me. Neither of us have left the house since we arrived. So, do tell how we're responsible for all of this yet you're the one with his blood on your shirt."

"Tesoro." He placed his hand on her shoulder, comforting her as he watched Vic.

"Nonna called a little after three o'clock this morning, he was still at the restaurant, drunk from the sounds I could hear in the background. She didn't know what to do with him. Jeff, her bartender, left and she was alone. Ale was saying crazy things. She was afraid."

"Is Nonna okay?" She reached up placing her hand over Jax's.

"A little shaken up but she's okay now that she's at home with her husband and son. They'll take care of her." Vic glanced back to Jax. "Jorge was pulling away when I got there. Nonna claims he killed Ale."

"Jorge?" Jax glanced to Finn. "Contact Pedro, find out what he knows. If I need to I'll make the drive back over to find out what he knows."

"This could mean the deal is off." Finn warned. "Want me to call some of the other guys?"

"Not yet." He didn't want to stir up any problems before they knew all the details.

"Papa...he's really..." Her voice broke and Jax wrapped his arms around her waist as her legs gave out. "But we were going to fix this..."

"I'm sorry, Tesoro, so sorry." Supporting her weight, he brought her

66

further into the living room, toward the sofa. "Sit with us Vic, finish telling us what you know."

"Ale was still alive when I arrived. Nonna by his side, holding his hand, when I joined them. He kept mumbling about you and Pedro. He asked me to make sure I got you back from Pedro, to make sure his grandchild wasn't raised by those monsters. Kaytlyn…are you with child?"

She let out a light laugh before shaking her head. "No. Papa made a deal that I'd carry Pedro's child in exchange for papa's life. Thanks to Jax that isn't my fate any longer."

"I was able to bring her home on good faith that I would kill Ale. If I failed he'd come for her. This change…" He glanced at her before continuing. "I'll keep you safe."

"We'll keep you safe. You're family, Kaytlyn, like a daughter to me. I've failed my own children but I won't fail you. Come back to the house, you'll be safe there." Vic glanced at Jax. "Both of you."

"No." She answered before Jax could. "Uncle Vic, I want a life of my own. I don't want to be a prisoner in my own home again. I got into law school, I want to go. I want the life I dreamed of. I don't want to be the family lawyer, getting the guys out of trouble every other day. I'll be there for you and our immediate family, for those who I consider family but I can't be part of the family business."

"You'll still be in danger because of who you are, who your father was."

"I'll keep her safe." Jax assured him. "I want Kaytlyn to marry me. She'll be my wife and my responsibility."

"I assume that means you're not rejoining the family now that you're out of prison." Vic shook his head. "Kaytlyn, you're family so I'll allow you to take two of my best guys with you. I've trusted Jax and Finn for years and I know they'll keep you safe."

"Damn right we will." Finn added coming back into the room. "Pedro will be here at eleven to discuss the matter with you. All he'd say for sure is the matter had been dealt with, he'll explain more upon his arrival."

"There is much I need to attend to." Vic rose. "There will be an autopsy but Kaytlyn, I'd be honored if you allow me to handle the funeral arrangements. Ale and I might not have seen eye to eye over the last several years but he's my brother and your father, we loved him. He was the head of this family for years and his funeral needs to reflect his status. A proper farewell to give us all closure."

"Thank you." She stood and went to her uncle. "I know you'll go back to the house and begin to join the family together after this. Please don't let Papa's way of ruling continue. You're better than that. The family can be much better under you. I'm not suggesting going legal because I know that will never happen but remember what happened to Sig and Gianna. To me. We were pawns in my father's bigger plan."

"I'll remember." He wrapped his arms around her, bringing her in for a quick embrace. "If I ever forget, you'll be around to remind me."

"Always." She nodded. "I'll do whatever I can to help you build the family in a stronger way."

Jax stood back allowing them to have their moment. He knew after Vic left that Kaytlyn would need him. She'd grieve for her father, for the man she loved, and for the man who betrayed her. Then she'd move on and live the life she always wanted. *A life with me hopefully.*

Chapter Twelve

"So, what's this about being your wife?" Kaytlyn leaned against the bedroom door, watching him as he stripped off his clothes. It had been a long day and both of them were exhausted, but she wasn't ready to sleep yet. Every second of the day had been trying, physically and emotionally draining, she needed something to replenish herself. She needed him.

"Ahh yes." He tugged his shirt over his head. "I want you as my wife, as the mother to my children. Though how will it look with you a lawyer and me a criminal."

"Former criminal." She reminded him stepping away from the door. "You might have a record as long as my arm, but you could put it behind you if you wanted."

"Who said I want to?" He reached out, looping his arm around her waist, and drawing her close. "You fell in love with this bad boy, changing now could mean we lose our spark."

"We could never lose that." Wrapping her arms around his torso she snuggled against him. This conversation had been weighing on her mind for hours. No matter how many times she played through how it could go she wasn't sure if it would turn out disastrous. Whatever happened, whatever the outcome, she'd deal with it. As long as she still had him in her life. "We both lost so much to this life. Maybe it's time we both move on."

"You have your life set out before you, you're going to start law school in a few months. What do I have to look forward to?"

"Don't you play that with me." She tipped her head to look up at him. "I know you always wanted to open up your own martial arts studio. There's no reason you couldn't do that. On the drive through East Aurora's main street I noticed a couple empty business fronts, surely one of those would have the space you need. You and Finn, you could do it."

"Maybe Finn, he has a pretty clean record, but not me. No one wants their children to be taught by a criminal."

"My black knight, you're turning your life in a different direction. There's no better teacher out there. Trust me I should know. I couldn't defend myself from a fly before you came into my life and now I'm better but...well thankfully I have you and Finn."

"Don't sell yourself short. You put up a good fight with Jorge. I had my money on you before he slammed your head against the trunk." He slipped his hands under her shirt. "It's been a hell of a day. Why don't we put the talk of the future aside until tomorrow? Tonight I think shower sex is in order. What do you say, will you join me in the shower?"

"Go heat it up, I'll be right there." She leaned back tugging her sweater over her head before he finally let her go.

"It will be hot enough." He slipped his hand into hers, dragging her long to the bathroom with him.

Moments later she was locked in his embrace, water cascading down their naked bodies. Her hands roamed over his body, taking in the new muscle, while her gaze stayed focused on his face. Even with the loss of her father still fresh, she was grateful to have him by her side. It was like a dream come true to be standing there with him.

Every time his touch left her body, she felt a chill rush through her. She longed for their next embrace, even a simple caress. He was like the air in her lungs, she couldn't live without him. She'd spend her life with him if he allowed her. It was what she wanted more than even going to law school.

Her arm brushed along the cool glass shower door, causing her to shiver, and he turned toward her. "Ready?"

"Always ready when it comes to you." Steam rose from the stall as he pulled her further into the cascade of water. Hot water flowed down her body, nearly scalding her. "Wow!"

"Too hot?" He shifted his body in front of hers, allowing his back to catch most of the spray. "Let me turn it down."

"No, leave it." She stopped him as he reached back for the handle. "Kiss me."

Not having to be asked again, his lips crushed against hers with such force she'd have stumbled if he hadn't wrapped his arms around her waist. Full of promise and desire, the kiss made her sink into his embrace. Even after multiple rounds of sex it was as if they still couldn't get enough of each other. Would it always be like this? A relationship was full of heat and desire in the bedroom and even more outside of it.

His tongue invaded her mouth. She was met with the spiciness of coffee he downed like water throughout the day. Before her thoughts could turn to

71

anything else, his hands ran down her body, exploring her curves. Slowly, he worked along her skin before sliding his hand between her legs. As his finger caressed her clit, sending waves of pleasure through her, she couldn't stop the moan from escaping around his unrelenting kiss. He worked his fingers inside of her, as his thumb continued to tease along her clit, pleasuring her in ways she only imaged. Breaking the kiss, he pulled his hand away and lifted her off the ground. He pressed her back against the cool tiles and kissed along her neck. "So fucking beautiful."

Wrapping her legs around him, she let her hands roam over his back. His shaft teased along her most intimate parts making her grind down against him. While he always made foreplay worth it for her, she wanted him inside of her. Teasing her nails along his back, she arched into him as he sucked her nipple between his lips, gently tugging until a moan tore from her lips. "Please…I want you. Now."

"Tesoro, you've always had me. You always will. Always." He let her nipple slip from his lips and rose so his face was inches from hers.

The way his fingers dug into her hips and his eyes stared into hers, she realized there was more to his comment than she understood, but before she could question it, he distracted her. Sliding his shaft along her folds, he teased along her opening before he slipped his hand between them. Readjusting, he thrust inside her with one continuous motion. Her head tipped back as another moan tore from her.

Buried to the hilt inside of her, he paused and pressed her tight against the wall. "I can't get enough of you. Most of the day I thought about doing just this. I love the way your body reacts to mine with the simplest touch. The way you eye me across the room, as if wanting me as much as I want you."

Any doubt that might remain he'd wake up and realize he'd made a mistake disappeared as she brought her hand from his back to cup the side of his face. "I love you, Jax."

With his eyes closed, he tipped his head forward, pressing his forehead against hers. "I love it when you say that while I'm buried balls deep in you."

Slowly his hips pumped against her, working his shaft in and out of her. With each pump, his pace sped until she arched into him, matching his thrusts with her own. With her fingers still tangled in his hair, she kept his face close, watching his eyes as he drove into her.

"Don't stop." She tipped her head back, letting it rest against the tiled wall of the glass-enclosed shower as her ecstasy grew. His own grunts kept pace with her moans. "Oh, Jax!"

He grabbed hold of her hips and drove his shaft into her harder and faster. The frenzy had her moaning until she called out his name and groaned as her climax sent her over the edge. He followed her moments later as he buried himself deep within her one final time.

"Fuck, Tesoro." He dipped his head to her neck, planting soft kisses along the curve before working his way up to her ear. "That was too quick."

"Don't." She pressed her finger to his lips. "After today we needed that and who said we were done. We'll finish this shower and who knows. A little sleep, some more lovemaking. We've got the rest of our lives."

Chapter Thirteen

Weeks flew by in a rush as Kaytlyn prepared for her first semester of law school while Finn and Jax put the final touches on their martial arts studio. Everything was coming together. Finn was still staying at the house with them to keep an eye on things as Uncle Vic was moving the family in a better direction.

Her black knight might have stayed on a law-abiding path, but he was still her bad boy. There were parts of him that would never be squeaky clean, just as there were parts of her. Maybe that was why they fit together as they did. They each came from a dark world and made their way into a semi gray area of life. It would never be black and white for them. Hell, she didn't want it to be. She needed a little excitement in her life, even if that was only having sex in the middle of the park where anyone could stumble upon them.

"Mail call." Jax called as he stepped through the front door, stopping snow off his boots. "There's something here from Gianna."

"What?" She dropped the law book she had been reading onto the coffee table and jumped off the sofa. "I've been emailing and writing to her for months with no reply."

"Well this is her handwriting." Jax held it up just out of her reach. "Give the delivery boy a kiss and you can have your letter."

"That's blackmail." She teased rising up onto her toes to press her lips to his. "Now give me the letter."

With the envelope in hand she slid her finger under the seal, careful not to destroy the envelope. Her heart raced in her chest as she pulled the folded stationary from the confines.

Dear Kaytlyn,

I apologize for the delay in responding. I bet you're frightfully worried, but I assure you everything is fine. Pavel and I are quiet well. We were traveling, he wanted to show me his home country. It was amazing and brought us closer together. I can honestly say I've never been happier in my life. It comes as a surprise to me as well. Uncle Ale thought he was doing this to bring peace to the families and he might have but he also gave me freedom.

Pavel is a kind and gentle man. I admit I was terrified of him at first, but over time I've grown to love him. His father still terrifies me, but I know my Pavel, he'll never let anything happen to me.

I can't wait for you to meet him. We'll be in the states in three weeks. I haven't told Papa yet, I want it to be a surprise. I need to tell him the news in person.

As I wrote this letter, I hadn't planned on telling you, but I can't help myself. We were close all our lives so it's only right I tell you now. I'm pregnant. Please don't tell anyone. Pavel and I agree if it's a boy we're going to name him Sigismondo, after my brother. Sigismondo Pavel Kuznetson. Quite a name, I know, but after the two most important men in my life.

There's so much more to tell you but I want to get this packaged before the mail leaves.

76

Also, I've established a new e-mail address GKuznetsov@Kuznetsov.com. That's the best way to reach me.

I'm sorry about Uncle Ale. I'd like to say I'll miss him but…

Love your cousin,

Gianna

"She's pregnant and in love." She leaned back against the back of the sofa. "I thought she'd be miserable and here she is happy and in love. I'm so happy for her."

"Then why are you crying?" Jax rubbed a hand down her arm.

"It's a woman thing." Finn shook his head. "Wait until she's pregnant. It will be water works for nothing more than a flower blooming in the garden."

"Hey." She snatched one of the throw pillows of the sofa and flung it at him.

"How do you know so much about it?" Jax eyed him.

"Girl I was dating, lived with her pregnant sister. It was a trip being there during her good mood swings. Other times you wanted to be as far away from her as possible." Finn shifted in the chair, placing the pillow she'd thrown at him behind his back. "Though she was also going through withdrawals so I'm sure that didn't help. She wanted to stay clean to give the baby a chance."

"And?" She pried wanting to know it worked out.

"Delivered a healthy baby boy, which was adopted. Two weeks later, the mother overdosed."

"Well fuck." Jax caressed along her hip.

"She stayed clean to give birth to her son. That has to count for something." Still it pained her to know the young woman was dead. The boy was adopted but if he ever sought out his birth mother it would be a dead end, or more to the point lead only to a grave.

"Tesoro, what's on your mind?" Jax took her hand into his and she glanced up at him.

"Seems like dead bodies litter the road of our lives. So many lost in senseless violence or drugs. When I was a young girl, I thought there were flowers and rainbows around every corner. Now I know the world holds so much darkness. Not even the brightest flashlight can shine through it sometimes."

"Two of the brightest flashlights can make an impact." He squeezed her hand.

"Three." Finn shot them a grin. "You're not getting rid of me. We're like a trio, someday with the right girl a foursome. We're in this together."

Together. That sounded perfect. Sometimes you have to travel through hell in order to find your piece of heaven. I'm not giving mine up.

Marissa Dobson

Marissa Dobson is a USA Today Bestselling Author of more than sixty books in different genres of romance, including Alaskan Tigers series.

Being the first daughter to an avid reader gave her the advantage of learning to read at a young age. Since then she has always had her nose in a book. It wasn't until she was a teenager that she started exploring writing.

Marissa lives an hour from Washington D.C. with her supportive husband, Thomas—who puts up with all her quirks and listens to her brainstorm in the middle of the night—and her writing buddy Pup Cameron, a cocker spaniel.

Also by Marissa Dobson

Alaskan Tigers:

Tiger Time

The Tiger's Heart

Tigress for Two

Night with a Tiger

Trusting a Tiger

Alaskan Tigers Box Set Vol. 1

Jinx's Mate

Two for Protection

Bearing Secrets

Tiger Tracks

Healing the Clan

Alaskan Tigers Box Set Vol. 2

Her Black Tiger

Tiger Trouble

Alpha Claimed

Roaring to be Claimed

Forever Creek Shifters:

Forever's Fight

Protecting Forever

Crimson Hollow:

Romancing the Fox

Loving the Bears

A Lion's Chance

Swift Move

Purrable Lion

Bearly Alive

Saved by a Lion

Furever Mated Box Set

SEALed for You:

Ace in the Hole

Explosive Passion

Operation Family

Marine for You:

Lucky Chance

Back from Hell

A Marine's Second Chance

Phantom Security:

Different Sides

Undercover Agent

Takeover Agent

Cedar Grove Medical:

Hope's Toy Chest

Destiny's Wish

Leena's Dream

Cedar Grove Medical Box Set

Fate:

Snowy Fate

Sarah's Fate

Mason's Fate

As Fate Would Have It

Half Moon Harbor Resort:

Learning to Live

Learning What Love Is

Her Cowboy's Heart

Half Moon Harbor Resort Vol. 1

Tanner Cycles:

Until Sydney

Stormkin:

Storm Queen

Blessing Montana:

Smoke

Touch of Home

United Homefront Ranch:

Destination Heaven

Beyond Monogamy:

Theirs to Treasure

Reaper:

Touch of Death

Clearwater:

Winterbloom

Unexpected Forever

Losing to Win

Christmas Countdown

The Surrogate

Clearwater Romance Volume One

Small Town Doctor

Stand Alone:

Road to Kaytlyn

SEALed Rescue

Past Comes to Light

SEALed Outcome

Starting Over

Secret Valentine

Restoring Love

www.ingramcontent.com/pod-product-compliance
Lightning Source LLC
Chambersburg PA
CBHW020639130626
46552CB00003B/1314